Within the fairy-tale treasury which has come into the world's possession, there is no doubt Hans Christian Andersen's stories are of outstanding character. Their symbolism is rich with character values. From his early childhood in the town of Odense, Denmark, until his death in Copenhagen, Hans Christian Andersen (1805-1875) wrote approximately 150 stories and tales. The thread in Andersen's stories is one of optimism which has given hope and inspiration to people all over the world. It is in this spirit that the Tales of Hans Christian Andersen are published.

A GIFT FOR HANS
by Hans Christian Andersen
Translated from the original Danish text by Hans
Henrik Breitenstein
Illustrated by Chris Molan
U.S. Edition 1988 by WORD Inc., Waco. TX 76702
Text: © Copyright 1988 Scandinavia Publishing House,
Nørregade 32, DK-1165, Copenhagen K. Denmark
Artwork: © Copyright 1988 Chris Molan and
Scandinavia Publishing House
Printed in Hong Kong
ISBN 0-8499-8547-1

Hans Christian Andersen

A Gift For Hans

Illustrated by Chris Molan
Translated from the original Danish text
by Hans Henrik Breitenstein

WORD INC.
Waco, TX 76796

There once was an old estate owned by a noble young squire and his wife. Riches and blessings they had, pleasure they wanted, and they did many good deeds. They wanted to make everyone as happy as they themselves were.

4

On Christmas Eve a marvelously decorated Christmas tree stood in the old banquet hall, a fire was burning in the fireplace and branches of fir had been hung around the old paintings. Here the lordships and guests gathered, and there was singing and dancing.

5

The joy of Christmas had filled the servants' hall early in the evening. Here also stood a large pine tree with red and white candles burning, small Danish flags, paper swans and fishing nets made from colored paper which were filled with "goodies."

The poor children from the parish had been invited, each was accompanied by his or her mother. She did not pay much attention to the tree. Instead she looked at the tables with the gifts of wool and linen dresses and trousers. That was where the mothers and the older children looked. Only the very small children stretched out their hands towards the candles, decorations and flags.

The whole group arrived early in the afternoon and was served Christmas pudding and roasted goose with red cabbage. When the tree had been displayed and the gifts distributed, they each had a small glass of punch and apple dumplings.

Then they went home to their own poor
quarters and talked about the "good life,"
meaning the food, and inspected the presents
one more time.

Among them were Garden-Kirsten and
Garden-Ole, who were married, and earned
their living by tending the garden on the estate.
Each Christmas they received their fair share of
the presents. They also had five children, all
five of whom were kept well dressed by the
lordships.

"Our lordships are generous people!" they
said "But then, they can afford to be and they
enjoy it."

"Here are sets of good clothing for four
children," Ole said.

"But why is there nothing for the cripple?
They don't usually forget him, even though he
does not attend the celebration."

They were talking about the eldest of the children, whom they called the "cripple," although his real name was Hans.

When he was small, he had been the brightest and liveliest child, but then all of a sudden his legs had turned weak so that he could neither stand nor walk, and he had now been bedridden for five years.

"Well, I was given something for him," his mother said. "Although it is not much, only a book for him to read."

"Surely that will not make him fat," his father said.

But Hans was happy to have the book. He was a keen lad who liked to read, but he also spent time performing such work as his bedridden state would allow. He was very good with his hands and skillful. He knitted woolen socks, even whole blankets. The lady at the manor had admired and bought them.

He had been given a book of fairy tales. In it was much to read and much to think about.

"That sort of thing is no use in this house," his parents said. "But let him read, that will keep him occupied, he cannot knit socks all the time."

11

Spring came. Flowers and green plants started sprouting. This included the weeds, which might be what nettles are, even though an old Danish hymn describes them in this way:

If all earth's kings stood forth in row,
With all their power and glory,
They had not strength to make,
The smallest leaf on a nettle grow.

There was so much to be done in the gardens, not just for the gardener and his apprentices, but also for Garden-Ole and Garden-Kirsten.

"What a lot of drudgery!" they said. "No sooner have we raked the garden paths and made them nice and tidy, when they are at once stepped on again. There are so many visitors at the manor. It must be expensive! But then our lordships have great wealth."

"How odd the way things are distributed," Ole said. "The pastor says that we are all God's children, so why this difference?"

"It is all due to the Fall," Kirsten said.

12

They talked about this again in the evening, when Cripple Hans was lying in bed with his book of fairy tales.

Want, toil and drudgery had hardened the parents' hands, but also their judgments and opinions. They could no longer bear nor stand it, and they now talked themselves into being even more angry and gloomy.

"Some people get wealth and happiness, others only poverty! Why must the disobedience and curiosity of our first parents harm us? We would not have done as they did."

"Yes we would," said Cripple Hans all of a sudden. "It says so in this book."

"What does the book say?" his parents asked.

And he read them the old story of the woodcutter and his wife. They, too, had complained about Adam and Eve's curiosity which had caused their misfortune.

Then the king of the country came their way.

"Come home with me," he said, "then you shall live just as I do: seven courses of food and a dish for show. This latter is inside a closed tureen, and you are not to touch it, for then your good life will end."

"What could be inside that tureen?" the wife asked.

"That is none of our business," the husband said.

"Well, it is not that I am curious," the wife said, "I only wonder why we dare not raise the lid; it must be something delicious."

"Hopefully there is no mechanical connection," the man said, "so that a gun will go off and wake up the entire household."

"Ooh!" the wife said, and did not touch the tureen. But during the night she dreamed that the lid had lifted itself, and there came the smell of the loveliest punch, of the sort you get at weddings and funerals. In it lay a big silver coin with the inscription:

"If you drink from this punch, you will become the richest people in the world, and all other people will become paupers."

"That thing is far too much on your mind," her husband said in the morning.

"We could peek only ever so slightly," the wife said.

"Yes, only slightly," the husband said. And the wife lifted the lid very quietly. Then two nimble little mice jumped out and disappeared into a hole.

"Good night," said the king. "Now you can go home and lie down on your own bed. And now you may no longer blame Adam and Eve, for you yourselves have been just as curious and ungrateful!"

"How did that story get into the book?" Garden-Ole asked. "It is as though it was about us. It really makes one think."

The next day Hans's parents went back to work; they were burned by the sun and drenched to the skin by the rain. Inside their minds sullen thoughts kept gnawing at them.

That evening, after they had finished their porridge, they asked Hans, "Read us the story of the woodcutter once more."

"There are so many lovely stories in the book," Hans said.
"So many you have not heard."

"Well I do not care for those," said Garden-Ole. "I want to hear the one I know."

And he and his wife heard it again.

More than one night they returned to that story.

"It still cannot make everything really clear to me," Garden-Ole said. "Just as milk curdles, so it is with people. Some become fine cheese, others become thin watery whey. Some people have happiness in everything, sit at the high table all their days and know neither want nor sorrow."

Cripple Hans heard this. His legs were weak, but his mind was sharp. He read aloud to them from the fairy tale book. He read about "The Man without Sorrow or Want." Where was he to be found? Because found he must be.

The king lay ill and could not be cured except by putting on the shirt which had been worn by a man which could truly say that he had never known sorrow nor want.

The message was sent out to all the world, to all castles and manors, to all rich and happy people. But when one pried into men's lives, they had to admit to having known sorrow and want.

"I haven't!" said the pigkeeper, who sat in the ditch, laughing and singing. "I am the happiest man!"

"Give us your shirt, then," the messengers said, "and you shall receive half the kingdom as a payment."

But he had no shirt. Still he considered himself the happiest man alive.

"A fine fellow!" Garden-Ole exclaimed, and he and his wife laughed as they had not laughed in years.

Then the schoolmaster came by.

"How cheerful you are," he said, "that is rare in this house. Have you won a prize in the lottery?"

"Nothing of the sort," Garden-Ole said. "It was Hans who read to us out of the fairy tale book. He read about "The Man without Sorrow or Want," and the fellow did not even own a shirt. Each man has his own burden to bear, one is not alone in that. There is always a comfort in this."

"Where did you get the book?" the schoolmaster asked.

"Our Hans got it for Christmas over a year ago. The lordships gave it to him. You know, he likes reading, and he is a cripple. Back then we would rather that he had been given blue linen shirts. But this is a curious book, it somehow seems to answer your thoughts."

The schoolmaster picked up the book and opened it.

"Let us have the same story once more," Garden-Ole said, "I do not quite have it all in there yet. Then he must also read the one about the woodcutter."

These two stories were enough for Ole. They were like two sunbeams shining into the poor room, into the subdued thoughts which had made him sullen and grumpy.

Hans read the entire book, and read it several times.

The stories carried him out into the world where he could not go since his legs could not carry him.

The schoolmaster sat by his bed; they talked and they both enjoyed it.

From that day on, the schoolmaster visited Hans more often when his parents were away working. The boy thought it was like a party every time he came. How he listened when the old man told him about the size of the earth and its many countries, and that the sun was almost half a million times bigger than the earth, and so far away that a cannonball, at its own speed, would take twenty-five years to travel the distance from the sun to the earth, while the rays of light could reach the earth in eight minutes.

Any clever schoolboy knows about that, but to Hans it was new and even more wonderful than what was in the fairy tale book.

A couple of times each year the schoolmaster was invited to dinner at the manor, and on one such occasion he told the lordships about the impact the book had had in the poor house, where merely two stories had brought such revival and blessing. The weakly, clever little boy had by his reading brought new understanding and joy into the house.

When the schoolmaster left the manor, the lady put a couple of silver coins in his hand for young Hans.

"Father and mother can have them!" said the boy when the schoolmaster brought him the money.

And Garden-Ole and Garden-Kirsten said "Even Hans the cripple is of use and a blessing."

A few days later, while his parents were away working at the manor, the lordships' carriage pulled up outside. It was the good lady who came, happy that her gift had brought such comfort and joy to the boy and his parents.

21

She brought fresh bread, fruit, and a bottle of sweet juice, but what was even more exciting, she brought him a little black bird in a golden cage that could whistle delightfully.

The cage with the bird was placed on the chest of drawers across from the boy's bed so that he could both see the bird and hear it. In fact, even people walking along the country road could hear its singing.

Garden-Ole and Garden-Kirsten did not arrive home until the lady had left. Even though they saw how happy Hans was, they thought the bird was a very inconvenient present.

"Rich people do not think so much," they said. "Now we must look after this one, too. After all, Cripple Hans cannot do it. In the end the cat will take it."

emperor and she became that, too. But then she wanted to become God Almighty, and suddenly she was back in the miry ditch from which she had come.

This story had nothing to do with the cat or the bird, but this was the story Hans was reading when the event took place. He would remember it forever.

The cage was on its chest of drawers, the cat was standing on the floor staring at the bird with his greenish-yellow eyes. There was something new in the cat's face, as though it wanted to say to the bird, "How lovely you are. I could eat you!" Hans understood. He read the cat's face.

Eight days passed, and yet another eight; during that time the cat had been in the room many times, without frightening the bird, let alone harming it. Then something extraordinary happened.

It was in the afternoon. His parents and the other children were out working. Hans was all alone. He held the book in his hands and read about the fisherman's wife, whose wishes were all fulfilled. She wanted to become king, and she became king. She wanted to become

"Go away, cat!" he shouted. "Get out of this room!"

The cat seemed to prepare a jump.

Hans could not reach it and had nothing to throw but his dearest treasure, the fairy tale book. He threw it, but the cover was loose, and it fell to one side, while the book with all its pages fell to another. The cat went a few slow steps back and looked at Hans, as if to say: "Do not interfere, little Hans. I can walk, and I can jump, but you can do neither."

Hans watched the cat and was very distressed. So was the bird. There was no one nearby to call for help. It was as if the cat knew. It prepared a second time to pounce. Hans waved his blanket, for he could use his arms. But the cat was not frightened by the blanket. When Hans had thrown that at the cat, too, but to no avail, it leaped onto the chair, up on the windowsill, and was now nearer to the bird.

Hans felt his blood rising, but he did not think about this, he only thought about the cat and the bird. He could not lift himself out of bed, and could not stand on his legs, much less walk. It was as though his heart turned inside him when he saw the cat jump from the windowsill to the chest of drawers and push the cage so it

fell over. The bird flapped wildly about inside. Hans let out a yell, a jerk went through his body, and without thinking about it, he jumped out of bed towards the chest, tore the cat away and held the cage with the terrified bird. He held the cage in his hand and ran out of the door and out onto the road.

Then tears started running from his eyes. Joyfully he shouted out loud, "I can walk! I can walk!"

He had regained the use of his legs. These things do happen, and it happened to him.

The schoolmaster lived nearby. Hans ran into his house wearing only his shirt and a sweater, and holding the cage with the bird.

"I can walk!" he shouted. "O Lord, my God," and he sobbed and cried for joy.

And there was rejoicing in the house of Garden-Ole and Kirsten.

"A happier day we could never see!" they both said.

Hans was called up to the manor. He had not walked that way for many years. It was as though the trees and nutbushes, those he knew so well, nodded to him and said "Hello Hans, welcome back!" The sun shone on his face and right into his heart.

The lordships, the kind young squire and his wife, let him sit with them. They looked just as happy as if he were one of their own family.

Happiest of all, however, was the lady, who had given him the fairy tale book and the little song bird. The bird had died of fright, but it had been the means of his healing and the book had been an inspiration to him and his parents. He still had the book, and would keep and read it no matter how old he grew. Now he could also be of some use at home. He wanted to learn a craft, preferably book binding, "because," he said, "then I can read all the new books!"

Later in the afternoon the lady called for Hans's parents to come up to see her. She and her husband had been talking about Hans. He was an honest and well-behaved boy, enjoyed reading and was bright. God always helps a good cause.

That evening the parents returned to the farm very happy, especially Kirsten. But a week later she cried, for it was time for little Hans to leave. He was nicely dressed. He was a good boy. But now he was to cross the salty waves, far away, attend school and learn Latin. It would be many years before they saw him again.

He did not take the fairy tale book with him, his parents wanted it for a remembrance. His father often read in it, but only from the two stories, because he knew those.

And they received letters from Hans, the one more cheerful than the other. He was staying with nice people, and was well off, and best of all, was attending school. There was so much to learn and know. All he now wanted was to live to be a hundred years of age and become a schoolmaster.

"If only we will live to see that!" his parents said and held hands just as they did when going to Communion.

"Think of what has happened to Hans," Ole said. "The Lord does consider the poor man's child. Imagine this should happen to the cripple. Isn't it as though he were reading it to us out of the fairy tale book?"

Explaining the story:

This story was one of Hans Christian Andersen's last ones. He believed it was one of his best. From it we learn that when we look at the circumstances around us—however hopeless they may seem—we must beware of our attitude. A complaining attitude compels us to compare ourselves to those better off than us. Soon we feel envious and bitter. We cut ourselves off from the miracles coming our way.

For those who have a thankful heart regardless of circumstances, there are miracles to discover around every new corner. When we forget about ourselves as Hans did, we make room for healing.

Talking about the truth of the story:

Give some examples of Garden-Ole's and Garden-Kirsten's negative attitudes.

Within this story, three shorter stories are told: "The Woodcutter and His Wife", "The Man without Sorrow or Want," and "The Woman in the Muddy Ditch." What does the first one tell us of man's nature? What does the second one tell us of the relation between suffering and happiness? What does the third one teach us about greediness? Which two stories are alike?

Why did the handicapped boy's parents want to hear only the two stories they already knew?

What three gifts did Hans receive from the mistress at the manor house? Which one did he like the best? Which one did his parents like the best?

Applying the truth of the story:

In contrast to the parents of the boy, what should our attitude be?

Though we may not be physically handicapped like Hans, we may be emotionally crippled as the short stories show. How can we find healing?

An old proverb says, "A cheerful heart is good medicine, but a crushed spirit dries up the bones".